TALES OF THE SUPERNATURAL
Fairy Stories

TALES OF THE SUPERNATURAL

Fairy Stories

by John Poulton

ROURKE PUBLICATIONS, INC.
Windermere, Florida 32786

Library of Congress Cataloging in Publication Data

Poulton, John, 1940-
  Fairy stories.

  (Tales of the supernatural)
  Summary: A retelling of sixteen classic
fairy tales, among them "The Firebird" and
"Hansel and Gretel."
  1. Fairy tales.   [1. Fairy tales.
2. Folklore]   I. Title.   II. Series.
PZ8.P86Fai   1982   398.2'1   82-10195
ISBN 0-86625-201-0

CONTENTS

A modern collection of fairy tales, full of fantasy
and enchantment, laughter and surprises.

Story One

The Remarkable Cat

There once was a giant who terrorized the country-
side for miles around. He ate the villagers' cows and
sheep for his dinner, and even the villagers themselves,
if he could catch them. And whenever he needed some
exercise he would go out and destroy a castle or two.
Houses and cottages he squashed just for fun. People
had to live like worms in underground tunnels to
escape his clumping feet and gnashing teeth.

At first they tried all sorts of ways of destroying
the menace. Regiments of archers fired at him, but the
giant merely turned himself into a huge tortoise so that
the arrows bounced off without hurting him at all. A
knight, braver than the rest, charged at him with a
lance, but the giant turned into a big black cloud and
the man sailed straight through him. Then the giant
changed back again and ate both knight and horse,
spitting out the armor and using the poor man's sword
as a toothpick.

All in all, he was a very nasty piece of work.

The giant made his home in a vast cavern,
and its floor was soon strewn with the bones and other
ghastly remains of his victims. No living thing had
ever dared approach this fearful place, so the giant

was amazed when one morning a cat strolled in. It walked with a jaunty air until it was just in front of his massive boot. The giant was so surprised that he quite forgot to squash it with his foot.

"Good morning," said the cat.

"Bah!" said the giant. "It's only a little cat. Not even a decent mouthful! All skin and bones, cats are. I shall have to swallow you down in a single gulp."

"I should be honored to be breakfast for such a magnificent giant," said the cat. "But I have travelled many a long mile to see you and talk to you, so I hope you will not eat me just yet."

"Eh?" said the giant.

"The stories about you were almost true," replied the cat. "But you are even bigger, stronger, and more handsome than people say."

"Eh?" said the giant again.

"Yes," the cat continued. "I felt I just had to come and see you for myself. But tell me, is it also true that you can change yourself into any shape you want?"

"Oh!" said the giant. "Oh, yes, it's true enough."

"Then," said the cat, "as your greatest admirer, I wonder if you would do me a great favor before you swallow me. Could you show me how you change your shape?"

Now, the giant was not very bright and he was very vain. No one had ever admired him before and the cat had cleverly discovered his weakness. The giant leapt into the air with a mighty bound, but it was not his usual self that came down again. It was a roaring lion. The lion paced about lashing his tail

8

and the cat fled up the wall in terror. Soon the giant tired of being a lion and became a giant again.

"There!" he said. "Will that do?"

"Magnificent," said the cat. "And I count it a great honor that you should choose the noblest of my relations to change into. However . . ."

"Yes?" asked the giant.

The cat pretended to be embarrassed for a moment, but then continued, "Well . . . changing into something big is not really so clever as all that, is it? I've seen common wizards do it at fairs for a penny a time. They could do you a whale or an elephant or a hippopotamus or a lion, with no trouble at all." He paused as if to clean his fur.

"Go on!" shouted the giant. "What *is* clever then? Quick, tell me, for I can turn into anything I like, anything at all. Just try me."

"Oh," said the cat. "It's the little things that take real skill. A calf, for example, or a squirrel, or . . . but no . . . surely even you couldn't become so small a thing as . . . no, that would be asking too much."

"Tell me, tell me this minute! Tell me what you were going to say!" bellowed the giant, angry that the cat could imagine that there was something he could not do.

"I was going to say 'a mouse', but of course I would understand if that's too small for you to manage."

"Just you watch!" yelled the giant, jumping into the air again. And sure enough when he came

down this time it was as a little grey mouse.
The cat killed it, of course.

The Fisherman's Mermaid

Many years ago on an island far to the north-west lived a fisherman with his wife and their baby daughter. Their cottage was hidden away behind the top of a high cliff and only a narrow crumbling path led down to the cove where the fishing boat was kept. Sadly, it was from this path that their first child had fallen to her death. The couple were so afraid that their second little girl would also tumble down the cliff that, from the moment she first began to crawl, they never let her out of the cottage. She grew up in the dim summer light and the winter firelight of the little stone house.

When the girl was six years old the fisherman's wife died. Some say she died from pneumonia and some say her death was caused by the evil black tobacco which she smoked from dawn till dusk in her black pipe. The fisherman buried her behind the cottage and planted bear berries on her grave. They never grew well, away from the mountain where he had found them.

Now there were only two in the cottage, and the poor man lived in fear of what might become of his daughter. He dreamed of her falling headlong down the cliff while he was away fishing, or being sucked into the bog, or attacked by ravens. In his despair he thought of a plan. He would tell his daughter stories of such terror and wonder about the world outside that she would never dare so much as to open the door. He started with what he could recall of the tales his granny had told him when he was young. When he could not remember details, he invented horrors. Soon he was bringing back from the mainland pictures and story-books which told of dragons and foul beasts of all descriptions. When the story had a happy ending he would tear out the last few pages and tell his daughter that the hero's fate was too awful for her to hear. All these dreadful things he told her as if they were real and perfectly true. Soon the girl was so afraid she would not even go near the windows, for fear that some monster would reach inside with its claws and seize her by the hair.

The fisherman filled the window-frames almost to the top with turf so that she could no longer see the world outside. One day, in great puzzlement, the girl asked her father a question which, for a moment, he was at a loss to answer.

"Father, since the world outside is full of terrors and miseries of which you never cease to warn me, how can it be that you yourself go out every day and return to me safe and sound with never so much as a scratch or a bruise?" The fisherman's mouth fell open in astonishment. So simple a question had never occurred to him and a truthful answer would mean the end of his plans. At last, he thought of a way out of his dilemma.

"Darling daughter," he said. "It is time that you learned that your father is no ordinary man. From my earliest youth I have battled against the evils of the world, and of this island in particular. Never have I been defeated and my strength and power are such that there is no monster, no demon, no dragon here that does not regard me with fear and dread. Fearing me so much, they flee when I approach, troubling me not at all when I go to catch the beautiful fishes of the sea. But they hate me! Oh, how they hate me! They would like nothing better than to catch you outside when I am away. That way they could hurt me without having to face me. But I am king of this island, and so long as you obey me and never venture outside, they are powerless. Your dear father is a great king. You have never seen my crown because I keep it hidden under a rock by the sea, for the ravens, who are my sworn enemies, would love to steal it."

Having told this dreadful lie, he found that he rather liked the idea and invented more, even worse lies. In a manner of speaking he *was* king of the island, but only because no one else would live there. You can be sure that he never told her that!

So, the fisherman's daughter grew up and reached the age of fourteen without ever having stepped outside her home. Looking at her, her father realized that she was beautiful. True, she was very pale from being indoors all the time, but then so were the princesses of old, or so the stories said, and now he almost believed them himself. So he painted two antique chairs gold, and raised a stone platform inside the cottage. One was his, the king's throne, and the other was for his princess.

It was good that he was a skillful fisherman and caught many shining silver salmon in the shallows around the island. For these, he was always able to get a good price on the mainland, and with the money he was able to buy many things to make his lies seem real. He dressed his daughter in robes and jewelry, and though the jewels were false the girl believed they were real. She would sit happily on her throne, listening to her father's latest tale of dragons slain or demons thwarted by his cunning.

But now the girl's beauty had brought him another worry. He feared that news of it would spread abroad and that some handsome man would seek her out on his island and carry her off to marry her. When he thought of it, tears of grief and rage welled up in his eyes just as if this event had actually happened. In order to make still more sure that his daughter would never stray outside and be seen from some passing boat, he told her a new lie.

"My dear, there is one thing more you should know which I have kept from you until now. The very ground outside has been poisoned by the ravens and their allies, the gulls. It may be that you have seen them dropping their little packets of white poison and wondered about it. I must tell you that if so much as your foot were to touch the poisoned earth you would shrivel up and perish miserably."

14

The girl replied, "But Father, surely your courage and strength are no protection against poison?"

Not to be caught without an answer a second time, the fisherman was ready, and replied, "The truth is that I have been walking this island for so many years that it no longer has much effect on me. But for you, unused to it as you are, it would mean instant death. Then again, you will have noticed that I never stir outside without my sea-boots, and they are some protection. But even I have not escaped entirely. These lines which you see on my brow and about my eyes are signs that the poison is working within me. They mark me but cannot harm me."

The girl had noticed his advancing wrinkles of course, and was not to know that they come to all men with age and worry.

The fisherman had remained unconvinced that there was no way in which news of his daughter could reach the outside world, and began to dream that the ravens carried the tale with them on their flights between the islands.

At about this time the girl began to feel a restlessness which she did not understand. For the first time, her curiosity began to overcome her fear and she spent more and more of her lonely hours gazing out through the cracks above the turfed windows. She could just see the sea which her father called his Own Great Highway, and wondered what the little black shapes were that sailed across it from time to time. Sometimes she could hear the sound of the waves, and then the sea drew her curiosity even more strongly, and it was as if it called out to her in her dreams. She was never so afraid of it as she was of the land, because her father loved the sea and could never conceal his affection when talking about it. She saw the gleaming fish that he brought up the cliff path and thought that it must indeed be a marvellous place if it were a home for such glittering creatures. It never occurred to the fisherman that he might have left something out of his picture of terror and menace.

The fisherman had saved up for a long time for something very special for his daughter. He was going to have a crown made for her. It would not be of real gold of course, nor studded with real sapphires, emeralds and diamonds, but gilt and glass would seem just as wonderful to the girl. It would still be very expensive and take a long time to make, nor could such a thing be had at the nearest town on the mainland. He would have to travel a long way to find a suitable craftsman. Therefore, with a final tale of the terrors which lurked outside, he prepared his princess for his long absence. He made sure that she had an abundance of food and fresh water, locked the door, barred it on the outside, and set off. As he sailed away he suddenly felt a pang like a pain in his chest and turned back to look at his island, but it seemed the same as always. Thinking of the delight which would fill his daughter's eyes and the tale which he would have to invent when he returned with the gleaming crown, he turned again to search for his sea-marks ahead.

Within the stone cottage the days dragged. The girl's restlessness became worse. She pushed at the window turfs so she could have a better view, and finally the uppermost layer toppled over and fell to the ground outside. At first, she was scared by what she had done, but then with growing boldness she managed to put her whole head through the gap. Now she could see more of the world than she had ever seen before. It did not look so very frightening after all. The sun was bright and cheerful. Small birds sang nearby and there was a pleasant chirping from the grasshoppers round about. A bird with a grey head and bright pink breast alighted on the fallen soil and began to pick at it for small insects. Soon it was joined by many more birds and the girl was afraid that they would soon finish their feast and fly away, leaving her alone again. She therefore pushed still more turfs out of the window-frame, and though at first the little birds flew off, they soon returned to their unexpected treat. With a start, the girl realized that the hole was now big enough for her to climb out. For many minutes she thought about it and then, with a careful look to see that there were no ravens about, she climbed up. She did not have to step on the earth. She could stand safely on the turf she had pushed from the window.

The wind from the sea played with her hair and the salt smell teased her nostrils in the most delightful fashion, and best of all, down there, down the crumbling path, she could actually see the great ocean itself. It heaved and tumbled and hurled its white vapour high into the air above the rocks and raced happily up the pale sand of the fisherman's cove.

But, how to get there? If she stepped on to the ground she would surely wither up and perish. But she did not *have* to step on to the ground! With a smile on her face such as her father had never seen, she stooped and picked up a good-sized turf, which she placed a little farther towards the path. Then she stepped on to it, turned, and picked up another from behind her. This she put on the path itself, and in a moment she had reached it. Putting one turf in front of the other she slowly and carefully descended the path to the sea.

The sun was hot and at times she felt dizzy. The sound of the sea was loud, and the grasshoppers made a noise that sometimes seemed to come from within her head itself. She was very tired, but it had all been worth it. She now stood where the sea at the end of its rush could actually touch the turf on which she stood. Behind her, stretching way above the high-tide mark, were the deep impressions on the soft sand which she had made with the advancing turfs. They looked like the footprints of some vast sea creature.

Now the sea touched her feet. It tickled. It was cool but friendly. She was entranced. It rose to her ankles, to her knees, and then to her waist. Her best princess's dress billowed about her on the foaming water. She laughed and sank in it up to her shoulders. It took her breath away, but she did not care. She tore off such of her garments as she could and watched them carried away by the current. She was glad to see them go. She wriggled through the water which seemed to support her. She swam as if she had been born to swim, not as children do, flailing their arms as if to punish the wetness, but as she imagined a salmon would, with lazy wriggles of her whole body. When she opened her eyes beneath the water she saw clouds of swirling sand, but farther out it was as clear as green glass.

The seals watched her in amazement. What could this creature be?

"I would say it was a girl," said the oldest of them, "except that humankind never lasts so long down here. They splutter and thrash about in an ugly fashion, and then they die. That alone makes it unlikely that she is a girl – and then of course there is that tail . . . "

"What are you?" asked the seals.

The girl was frightened at first, but the seals seemed so friendly and polite that she at last replied, "I am a princess."

"That would explain it," said the oldest seal. "We knew you couldn't be an ordinary girl, because of your beautiful tail. I suppose all princesses have tails?"

"I have no tail," the girl began, but then she looked down and saw that she had.

It was indeed a beautiful tail, graceful like a mackerel's, but of course much longer and bigger. She did not understand, but she was delighted with it. She turned and swam, and her new tail sent her speeding forward like a dolphin, so that even the fastest of the seals could scarcely keep up with her. They played together all the day, and at night she made patterns as she sped through the warm luminous water.

The seals entertained her and taught her all she

19

needed to know about sea matters. She forgot all about her father, except one day when there seemed to be something pricking at her memory. She climbed out of the water on to a rock at the foot of some cliffs near a cove. She could see some sort of track leading up the cliffs and a rough stone house at the top. There was something about the place which seemed familiar, but she could not remember what it was. She remained for a few more moments combing her hair with a curiously shaped sea shell that a seal friend had found for her, and then she slipped back into the water. She would not come back.

Her father had returned. He had pulled his boat up on to the wet sand. He had turned and picked up a parcel from the boat and carried it carefully up towards the path. He had seen the turf prints above the tide-line. They looked like the tracks of some vast sea monster. With a cry of terror, he raced up the path, dropping the parcel as he went. When he reached the cottage he hurled the bar aside. At first he could not get the key into the lock, then he disappeared inside. There was silence, followed by a wail more mournful and more lonely than any gull might utter, and then again silence.

The fisherman went down the path to the sea, picking up his parcel as he went. When he reached the water's edge he hurled it as far as he could, and then he sat down with his head in his hands. Weeks later the seals found a small crown in the water, but thought little of it. The sea was full of marvels these days.

Some say that the fisherman still sits by the water's edge looking for his daughter, but that by now he has turned to stone. It is certainly true that there is one rock that looks remarkably like a sad-faced man in a sandy cove far to the north-west.

Meanwhile the mermaid, for that is what she was, enjoyed herself with her new friends, but when the water began to turn cold they became worried about her. She lacked their warm blubber overcoats and began to shiver and seek the warmer currents. Sadly they advised her to swim south for the winter, and to come back to them next year. They told her that if each day she swam towards the sun when it was at its highest point in the sky she would reach warmer waters, and of course they were right. It would have been better to have swum by the stars, but they had not had time to teach her about those, because there are so many and it takes years to learn about them properly.

So, the mermaid who had been an ordinary girl, and also a sort of princess, swam south. It took a very long time and she had many adventures on the way, but that's another story.

Story Three
The Frog

Once there was a princess who was as conceited as she was beautiful. No prince was good enough for her, she said, and no one but a prince could possibly do as a husband. Her father was in despair. Although he loved her, in his heart of hearts he knew that he would never have a moment's peace until she was safely married and off his hands.

One day, the Princess was in her own private garden in which there was a small frog pool. She was wearing her second-best green dress and her emerald crown. She called it her second-best green dress because, she said, she had never seen one fine enough to be her first-best. She was playing with the only thing she really loved – a ball, a perfect, shining sphere of pure gold. She threw it into the air and caught it time and again. At last she missed a catch and the ball fell with a loud plop into the pool. She cried and stamped her foot, but the ball was gone, deep and out of sight.

"Why are you making such an awful noise?" asked a voice.

The Princess looked up. There was no one there. Only a huge frog of deepest green which sat at the edge

of the pool, regarding her with its fiery red eyes. The princess turned up her nose in disgust.

"If you must know," she said, "my best ball has fallen into your wretched little puddle and is lost for ever."

"Not for ever," said the frog. "I am sure I can find it."

At once the Princess's manner changed. "Can you?" she exclaimed. "Then dear, good Froggie, bring it to me instantly!"

"What will you give me if I do?" inquired the frog.

"Anything!" replied the Princess. "I love that little golden ball more than all my other possessions put together."

"Well then," said the frog. "I shall not require anything expensive or difficult of you. All I ask is to be allowed to sit at your table and eat from your plate." The Princess shuddered to think of such an ugly, clammy thing sitting beside her and sharing her food, but then she remembered her precious ball and told herself that, after all, she need not keep her promise. So she agreed to grant the frog his request.

In a green flash the frog was gone and before a minute was over he reappeared, this time with the golden ball between his forefeet. The Princess snatched her toy and was gone, leaving the frog struggling after her, calling "Wait! Please wait! Remember your promise!"

That night, as she sat at her father's table, the Princess heard the great bell clang at the palace door. The King sent a servant to see who it was. Imagine the Princess's dismay when he returned carrying the huge frog! The frog whispered to the King for a long time and, as he did so, the King began to frown.

When the frog had finished, the King turned to his daughter. "It seems, my dear, that you have broken your promise to this poor animal," he said.

The frog nodded his head sadly.

"No matter," the King continued. "You can make amends now. Take it to your place, set it beside you, and feed it!"

The Princess shuddered with horror, but she knew better than to disobey her father. She did as she was told. When the frog had eaten his fill he thanked the Princess, bowed as best he could to the King, and hopped out of the palace.

The very next day the Princess, wearing her second-best dress of crimson silk and her ruby crown, was again playing in the garden with her favorite toy. As ill luck would have it, she soon missed the ball and dropped it once more into the pool. Again the frog appeared and asked what she would give for the return of the ball.

"Anything!" said the Princess. "Anything reasonable, that is."

This time, all the frog wanted was to sit at the table and to drink from her golden cup. The Princess agreed, but as soon as the golden ball was safely in her hands she raced away as fast as her legs could carry her.

Once again, sitting at her father's table that evening, the Princess heard the doorbell clang. She knew what was going to happen, of course. The frog was brought in and her father was even more stern than before. Without a murmur, she held her cup to the frog's squashy mouth and he drank from it. Satisfied, the frog thanked the Princess and the King, and hopped away.

On the third day the Princess, dressed in her second-best dress of white lace and her diamond crown, was playing by the pool. Not only was the Princess conceited, but stubborn as well. She was determined not to be driven out of her favorite garden just because it contained a frog pool. For half an hour she played without missing a catch, but then, just as she was congratulating herself on her cleverness, the ball struck her thumb and plummeted into the pool.

The frog was there instantly, as if by magic.

"Well! What do you want this time?" the Princess asked angrily.

"Nothing difficult," replied the frog. "Nothing expensive. I will return your ball to you if I may kiss your beautiful lips."

"What!" exclaimed the Princess. "Kiss a frog!"

"No kiss, no ball," answered the frog. The Princess thought for a moment, then a sly smile appeared on her face.

"I agree," she said.

In a few moments the frog had returned the ball and was sitting at the edge of the pool with his clammy lips puckered for a kiss. But the girl seized the ball and fled laughing up the path to the palace, leaving the frog sitting by himself with the strangest expression on his face. When the Princess reached the palace she stretched up to the doorbell. Then she wrapped her fine silk scarf round and round the clapper.

"There!" she said. "Ring as hard as you like, Froggie! This bell will never make a sound."

At the table that evening the Princess sat with a satisfied smile on her face. The dinner was served and there was no sign of the frog. The plates were cleared away by the servants, and still no frog! The King chatted to his daughter for a while and then, just as she was about to go off to bed, there came a tapping on the window. The Princess turned white. A servant opened the window and returned carrying the frog. The brave animal had climbed the ivy, even though his webbed feet were never meant for such a thing and the window was high above the ground. Panting, he told the King of the Princess's latest promise. The King's brow grew dark as thunder.

"My daughter!" he said sternly. "You must learn that promises are to be kept, whether made to a king or to a frog. Kiss him!"

The girl wept and pleaded with her father, but he would not relent. "Kiss him!" he demanded.

"Yes please," said the frog.

The Princess screwed up her eyes so as not to see what she was kissing and advanced to the cold creature. It planted a kiss on her lips with a mighty smack! The Princess opened her eyes. She stared, unable to believe what she saw. Her father was staring too, open-mouthed. Before them stood a young man dressed in green, every inch a prince, as was obvious to anyone.

He soon explained that he had been bewitched and turned into a frog long ago, and that only a kiss from a true princess could return him to his rightful shape.

Needless to say, the Prince asked the Princess to marry him, and of course she agreed. They decided that they would never tell anyone how they came to meet, but after they were married, if ever the Princess became conceited or stubborn, the Prince would stretch his mouth as wide as he could and say "Croak!"

That cured her!

Story Four
The Boy Who Sang

In a town by the sea lived a boy who could play the fiddle. He could sing and play at the same time. This is not easy, so he became famous for it. He did it so well that when he sang a sad song even tough old sailors would burst into tears, and when he played a happy tune sour old fishwives would dance and caper with silly grins on their faces.

At length, news of his playing reached the ears of the Prince. The boy was invited to play at the palace, and he was very nervous.

"The Prince won't like my simple songs," he said. "Why, he has a whole orchestra of his own whenever he wants music. He'll be cross with me and get one of his soldiers to break my fiddle over my head."

But the boy was wrong. Both Prince and Princess so liked his playing that they tried to give him money and grand presents.

The Prince said, "You can live here in the palace with my servants to look after you. You can eat at my table and I'll give you gold, which will keep you in luxury for the rest of your life."

But the boy replied, "Thank you, Highness. You are very kind, but I don't need all these expensive things. People are always very good to me and I'm never allowed to go hungry. But don't worry, I'd be delighted to play for you as often as you like."

The Prince and Princess were pleased that the boy was not greedy and made sure that he came to play at least three times a week. The three of them became great friends.

One of the boy's favorite pastimes was to sing and play to the creatures of the sea. He would sit on a rock at high tide and play while the slow waves crept green and deep all around him. The gulls and cormorants would wheel in silence round the rock, and the seals popped their heads out of the water to listen contently for hours. Best of all, and best loved by the boy, the dolphins would cease their leaping and tumbling to circle the rock slowly for as long as he continued to play. After each song they would twitter excitedly to each other like mechanical birds, but they fell silent the moment the music began again. The dolphins had their favorite songs, and when one of these was finished they would come half out of the water, clamouring with clicks and whistles till he played it again.

One day the boy heard of a music competition to be held in a city many miles distant. The finest musicians from many countries were to gather in order to compete for splendid prizes. The boy did not care about prizes, but thought he might enter the competition to see if he really was as good as the Prince and Princess had said. He told the Prince he wanted to go.

"Please don't leave us," begged the Prince. "It's hundreds of miles away. You would be gone for weeks and weeks. Whatever would we do without you?"

"Don't worry," said the boy. "I'll take the fastest ship there and the fastest ship back. I won't be gone long at all."

At these words the Princess turned quite pale. The mention of ships had frightened her.

"Do not say that," she said. "I have a strange feeling that for you ships mean nothing but evil. Don't ask why I feel this, for I don't know, but take my advice, never travel by sea. If you must go, you will have to go on foot and we'll just have to manage without you as best we can. But you must promise me that you will never venture aboard a ship or I will not allow you to leave the palace."

Bewildered by what the Princess said, the boy gave her his promise.

Carrying a large leather bag filled with delicacies from the Prince's kitchens, the boy set off on his long journey. The way led up mountainsides, over high passes, and through ragged ravines where icy wind leapt at his throat. Somehow though, he always managed to find shelter before night fell. When the food the Prince had given him ran out, there was always someone to feed him in return for a song or two. He came to like the hard cheese and grey bread which was the main fare in these parts.

At last, a wide sunny plain lay before him. A broad river flowed to the sea, and where river and sea met was the city in which the competition was to be held.

News of the boy who sang and played the fiddle had gone ahead of him and he was warmly welcomed. In the days leading up to the competition he made his living by entertaining the crowds who were flooding into the city. A certain old man listened to him every day. He wore two wreaths of old dry leaves on his head, and under his arm he carried a beautiful harp. The crowds applauded the boy, but the old man snorted angrily and shook his bearded face at them.

"Don't think the judges will listen to that simple rubbish," he said. "Feast your poor ears on this!"

Thereupon the old man started to play his harp and sing in a trembling, high-pitched voice. It was beautiful music, certainly, but the words were too complicated for the crowd to understand.

"There!" said the harpist when he had done. "That has won me the competition these last two years and it will win again this year, you mark my words."

Privately, the boy thought he was probably right.

The competition was held in a great open theater cut into a steep hillside overlooking the sea. The performers sang or played on a raised stage. Thousands had gathered and they clapped and cheered so loudly that it made the boy's ears hurt. Lots were drawn. He was to play last, immediately after the harpist. The applause for the old man went on and on, so the boy had to stand waiting till they had quietened down. The moment he began, the crowd was still. It seemed as if every single person was holding his breath.

When he had finished there came no sound at all from the audience. The boy was miserable. Oh dear, he thought. I think they might clap just a little bit, if only for politeness' sake.

And then they did – louder and louder. Then they all stood up as one man and let out such a roar of delight that the boy had to press his fingers into his ears.

There was quiet again while the judges decided who was the winner. They took a long time.

At last a messenger ran towards the waiting performers. The harpist stepped forward expectantly, but the messenger ran straight past him and stopped by the boy singer. He took him by the hand and led him back on to the stage. The crowd roared and cheered. The chief judge buckled a great jewelled belt about his waist and placed a wreath of fresh leaves on his head. He had won first prize!

The harpist came second and got a bag of gold, but no wreath and no jewelled belt. He scowled, spat and stamped, and left the platform in a fit of rage. But the winner had to play again and again. It was ages before he could persuade the crowd to let him go.

Now that the competition was over the boy had but one thought in mind: to get back to his friends, the Prince and Princess. But the judges refused to let him set off over the mountains again. They said that, now he had the belt, every robber in the country would be lying in wait for him. A ship was leaving soon and in any case it would be much quicker. He remembered the Princess's warning, but what could he do? He wasn't afraid. He decided to take the risk and go by sea.

He boarded the ship, his belt hidden in his leather bag for safe keeping. He made himself comfortable in his cabin without a care in the world. He would not have been so happy, however, if he could have seen what was going on above deck.

The old harpist was aboard, talking to the captain. There was much nodding of heads and a small bag of gold changed hands. The harpist slunk ashore with a nasty smile of satisfaction on his face. The captain hid the little bag in his tunic, glanced guiltily about him, and yelled for the crew to cast off. Soon the ship was away, speeding for the boy's home port with a brisk following breeze.

On the second day out the captain called for the boy.

"Well, my lad," he said. "I think you had better say your prayers quick, for I mean to have your fancy new belt and cut your throat."

The boy was amazed. He had never met such wickedness before.

"Take the belt if you wish, but why cut my throat? I haven't done you any harm."

"I'm not stupid," said the captain. "If I were to leave you alive you would tell your tale and I'd never be able to enter port again. I'd be arrested and hanged. Then what good would the belt be to me, eh? Say your prayers, I tell you, and be quick about it!"

Seeing the captain was in earnest, the boy hung his head. "If my life is to end so soon, let me sing one last song. It would cost you nothing and then I could die quite happily."

The captain was suspicious at first, but once he had his hands on the bag containing the belt, he agreed to the boy's request.

The boy made his way along the bowsprit, out over the rushing white water, and sat with his feet entwined in the ropes. Perched out there like a figurehead, he began to play and sing while the sea spray swept around him. The sailors crowded on to the fo'c's'le to listen. His last song was about the sea and his love for all sea creatures. It was his best song yet. He had just finished when the ship met a wave much larger than the rest. The salt water crashed over the boy and he lost his balance and toppled. The captain would not have to use his knife after all. He smiled, turned to his crew, and tipped the belt out on to the deck.

Down the boy fell. He hit the water and instantly the world turned a rushing green with swirling clouds of white bubbles. Over and over he tumbled, deeper and deeper, while the black shape of the ship's hull sped by above him. He opened his mouth to sing but the water filled his throat. This is the end of me, he thought. I hope the Princess never hears what has happened. I hope the dolphins will not be too sad....

It seemed to him that a dolphin appeared at that very moment, and then another. They circled him swiftly, closed in, and then he was borne upwards between the backs of the two grey creatures. There was a sudden explosion of light and his head was out of the water again. He choked and spluttered till the water left his lungs. He was surprised and delighted to be alive again. The dolphins twittered to him and one of them began to sink gently, allowing him to climb aboard the other. He reached back to grasp the dorsal fin. Then they were off!

The ship was swift but the dolphins swifter. The crew never noticed when they were overtaken by a boy on a dolphin. They were too busy sharing out gold and jewels from the belt.

Sometimes, when one dolphin tired, the boy had to climb on to another of the streamlined beasts, but by now the water was full of them, all waiting their turn to carry him home.

When at last he was safe and sound on the familiar shingle beach, he spoke to them.

"I can never thank you properly for what you have done. But I will always come and sing to you. I shall tell everyone how you saved me and I'll ask them never to hurt you. My friend the Prince will make a law and no one will dare harm you then."

The dolphins seemed to understand, so the boy set off to tell the Prince and Princess everything.

Two days later the ship arrived. With a face which he tried to make sorrowful, the captain began to tell a story about a passenger who sang to the sea and then fell overboard by accident and was drowned. He was most surprised when burly soldiers laid hold on him and his crew and carried them off to prison.

The boy did not see them go. He was out on the rock singing to the dolphins, a brand-new fiddle tucked underneath his chin. The dolphins never did find the old one.

The Truth Boxes

Once, while working in his stony field, a poor peasant dug up a golden horseshoe. He took it to his skinny old wife and said, "Look at this, my dear. It is gold and I hear tell that gold is precious stuff. Perhaps we could sell it for a good price."

His wife chuckled with excitement. "We will go to the city and see what they will give us for it," she said. Then her face fell. "But I hear that the people there are rogues. They might cheat us. We know nothing of city ways and we would fall for their tricks."

They both thought for a moment and then the man said, "I shall go to our neighbor. He knows the ways of the world and perhaps he will give us good advice."

This proved how simple the poor fellow was, for the neighbor was a villain who had made himself rich at the expense of the folk who lived nearby. When he saw the horseshoe gleaming in the poor man's hand he knew its value at once, and his eyes filled with greed. "You did well to come to me," he said, "for you would certainly have been cheated by the city merchants — or worse, knocked on the head by robbers, and your horseshoe stolen. Give it to me. I will take it to the city for you. I know the ways of the world and can get you a fair price for it."

The peasant handed the beautiful golden horseshoe to his neighbor and thanked him very much for taking so much trouble. The old man and his wife returned to their hut, believing that they had left the matter in good hands.

As soon as they were gone, the bad neighbor saddled his donkey and set off for the city as fast as the little animal could carry him. There, he sold the precious object for a great sum of money and then returned home as fast as he had left. The poor donkey was exhausted by the time they got back. The neighbor's face was a picture of evil happiness because he had thought of a way to keep the money for himself. With a mournful expression on his face, he went to find the peasant and his wife. They listened anxiously while he told them the story that he had invented.

"Ah, if only you had found your horseshoe *last* year!" he sighed. "A great gold-mine has been discovered right underneath the city and the citizens are hauling out gold by the cart-load every minute of the day and night. Gold is so common now that the King has ordered the buildings to be covered with the stuff, so that they shine in the sunlight. Children play with gold nuggets in the streets. The miners overload the carts, you see, and cannot be bothered to stoop and pick up the chunks which fall off. There is so much of it about that your golden horseshoe has no value any more. No value whatever."

The poor peasant and his wife believed all these lies and they were very sad.

The neighbor held out his hand in which were three copper pennies, and then continued, "But I did sell your horseshoe after all. I got these pennies from a man who said he would buy it for luck. When last I saw it, it was nailed to his dog's kennel."

The peasant took two of the coins. "Please keep the other," he said. "You had a wasted journey on our account and it will help pay you for your trouble."

Scarcely able to keep his face straight, the villain took his copper penny and ran home, congratulating himself on having such simple-minded neighbors. Once inside, and with his door securely barred, he poured out on the table the bags of money he had been given for the horseshoe. His wife, who was as plump as the peasant's wife was skinny, cried out in delight. She threw handfuls of the coins up into the air and told her husband what a fine fellow he was to bring home such wealth, and how clever he was to outwit those simpletons.

In their own little hut, those simpletons were talking.

"Never mind," said the wife. "Two copper pennies are more money than we have ever had before. How shall we spend them?"

Her husband looked puzzled. "I don't know," he said. "I have never had money to spend before. I don't know how to do it."

"I will tell you what I should like," replied his wife. "I should like to see this city which is covered with gold. It's such a pretty color and the place is sure to look lovely with the sun shining on it. We could spend our money there."

The old man was astonished. Neither he nor his wife had ever been far from the village before. Few people travelled in those days, so his wife's suggestion was a surprise.

"What a strange idea that we should go there, as we no longer have anything to sell," he said. But the idea appealed to him. "Wife!" he said. "We'll do it! We'll see this marvelous place that is covered with gold, with our very own eyes."

So they set off, there and then.

They had no donkey, so it was several days before they approached the city. All the time they searched the road ahead for signs of sunlight gleaming on golden roof-tops. The city appeared before them, but of course there was not a trace of gold to be seen. They stood before the main gate, puzzlement on their faces, while people bustled around them with never a glance for the peasant and his wife. At last they understood.

"Our neighbor has made fools of us," said the man as they wandered up and down the very ordinary streets. "He must have sold our horseshoe and kept the money for himself. To think, I even let him keep a penny for his trouble!"

"He never expected us to come and see for ourselves," said his wife. "But even though we now know that he has robbed us, there is nothing we can do. Who would take our word against his? He's sure to have thought up a good story to explain how he got the money."

At that moment a king's messenger stopped in the street. He blew several blasts on a trumpet and when he had his breath back, he called out in a loud voice, "Hear ye, hear ye citizens, hear the command of His Majesty, your king. His Majesty commands that all who desire justice present themselves before him tomorrow at noon. His Majesty himself will hear complaints, as is his duty. His Majesty himself will pass judgement. Hear ye, hear ye, hear ye."

Then the messenger was off again and his trumpet could be heard from time to time in the distance.

The peasant and his wife looked at each other.

"Dare we?" he asked.

"Yes!" she replied.

The couple were terrified when at last they were called before the King, but he spoke to them kindly and the peasant was able to tell the whole story.

"A difficult case," said the King. "If what you say is true, your neighbor is a villain indeed. But you will understand that he must be allowed to answer your charge for himself. It wouldn't be fair if I were to punish him without hearing *his* story as well, would it?" They agreed that this was only fair, so the King's servants were sent to fetch the neighbor, and the couple had to wait.

Some days later they were called to the palace, and there was the wicked neighbor and his fat wife whom he had brought along to help him with his lies. Standing on either side of the King were two of his ministers, one as small and skinny as the peasant and one as big and heavy as the neighbor. The King spoke quietly to them from time to time. At length, the little one called for the peasant and made him tell his story all over again. As he was telling it, his neighbor made indignant noises and waved his hands in protest. The little minister had to tell him to be quiet several times.

Then the neighbor had his chance to speak. He began, "Dear King, Your Most Noble Majesty, whose justice is praised to the four corners of the earth, I am sorry that you have been forced to listen to that pack of lies. This wretched man is lazy and he is jealous of my wealth which I have gained by honest hard work. It was *I* who found the horseshoe, and so of course the money I got for it is rightfully mine. As for that ridiculous story about the gold-mine which I am supposed to have told – well, who would have been taken in by such a tale, I'd like to know? He pretends to be simple, but no one is *that* simple! It's a crafty plot to rob me, Your Majesty. Don't believe him, I beg you."

The neighbor's wife then stood up and swore that all her husband had said was the honest truth, and that the poor peasant was a thief and a liar. The peasant looked at his own wife and shook his head sadly. Who was going to believe the true story now, he wondered.

Now that both sides had had their say, the King thought for a long time and consulted his ministers.

44

There was much shaking of heads and then the King spoke.

"We cannot decide who is telling the truth." Then he turned to his ministers and said, "Prepare the truth boxes."

The ministers bowed and departed. The King then turned back to the peasant and his neighbor.

"One of you is lying. I cannot tell which, but the truth boxes can. Come with me."

He led the men and their wives out into a large and beautiful garden. A chair had been placed there for him, and in front of it stood two large boxes, carved and painted, with carrying handles. They did not know what to make of them.

"Now," said the King, sitting down. "You and your wife," he began, pointing to the neighbor, "must take the righthand box and carry it around the garden in a clockwise direction." Then he pointed to the peasant and his wife and said, "And you, you must take the lefthand box and carry it around the garden in an counterclockwise direction. You may rest for a short while if you are tired, but do not come back here to me until I call you. Do you all understand?"

All had mystified expressions on their faces but they all nodded.

"Good," said the King. "Truth takes its time, but the truth I shall have if it takes all afternoon. Off you go!"

Bewildered, the couples picked up their boxes and staggered off in opposite directions round the garden. Though the villain and his wife were much the stronger, neither pair found it an easy task. The day was warm and the boxes heavy, and soon the sweat ran freely down their faces.

Pausing under an acacia tree at one end of the garden the peasant said to his wife, "I'm sorry to have got you into this, but we'll have to keep going until the King tells us to stop."

"Don't worry about me," replied his wife. "I cannot see how all this boxes business will help the King to make up his mind, but you told the truth so I'm sure all will be well in the end."

Meanwhile, at the other end of the garden, the neighbor and his wife had paused, puffing and panting, beneath a shady cedar tree.

"I'm sick of this," said the woman. "I would never have agreed to come and help you if I had known."

"Hush, woman!" replied the villain. "So long as we stick to our story we're safe. I know my tale was a lie, but who can prove it? Certainly not these boxes. Come on! Pick it up and let's be off again."

Round and round the garden went the pair, scowling whenever they met the other couple coming towards them.

At long last the King called a halt and the boxes were placed before him. "I will now consult the truth boxes," he said. "Go a little way off."

When they were too far away to hear, the King bent down as if listening first to one box then to the other. He seemed satisfied and called the couples back. Turning to the wicked neighbor he said, "You are the thief and the liar, and your wife is no better

47

than you are! You shall return the money you had for the horseshoe to this poor man, and then you shall see the inside of my dungeons for a year or two."

Protesting and begging for mercy, the deceitful couple were taken away.

Smiling, the King turned to the peasant and his wife, who were more amazed than ever, but were now beaming happily.

"All seems to be in order now. My servants will find the money and give it to you," he said. "I will keep those rogues locked up for a while and that should cure them. But if they cause you any trouble when they have been released from prison, come and tell me. I shall know what to do."

The couple thanked the King and then the peasant asked how he had discovered the truth.

"From the truth boxes, of course!" said the King, and then he sent them home, still mystified, but happy.

When they had gone, the King opened up the boxes. Out climbed the two ministers. The wicked neighbor and his wife had spent the afternoon carrying round the fat one while the peasant and his wife had been carrying the thin one. From their hiding-places they had heard every word uttered when the couples had paused beneath the trees, and of course they had whispered the truth to the King.